PEDRO

PEDRO KEEPS HIS COOL

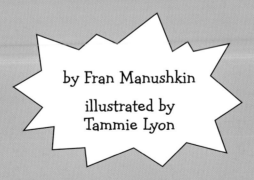

by Fran Manushkin

illustrated by
Tammie Lyon

PICTURE WINDOW BOOKS
a capstone imprint

Pedro is published by Picture Window Books,
a Capstone imprint
1710 Roe Crest Drive
North Mankato, Minnesota 56003
www.capstonepub.com

Library of Congress Cataloging-in-Publication Data
Names: Manushkin, Fran, author. | Lyon, Tammie, illustrator. | Manushkin, Fran. Pedro.
Title: Pedro keeps his cool / by Fran Manushkin ; illustrated by Tammie Lyon.
Description: North Mankato, Minnesota : Picture Window Books, [2019] | Series: Pedro | Summary: It is snowing, and Pedro and his friends go to the park to have some fun in the snow. His snow figure and snow angel are not successful, but Pedro knows he is a great sledder—and he is determined to help Roddy overcome his fear of sledding on the big hill.
Identifiers: LCCN 2019006310| ISBN 9781515844518 (hardcover) | ISBN 9781515845645 (pbk.) | ISBN 9781515844532 (ebook pdf)
Subjects: LCSH: Hispanic Americans—Juvenile fiction. | Snow—Juvenile fiction. | Sledding—Juvenile fiction. | Friendship—Juvenile fiction. | CYAC: Hispanic Americans—Fiction. | Snow—Fiction. | Friendship—Fiction.
Classification: LCC PZ7.M3195 Pce 2019 | DDC 813.54 [E] —dc23
LC record available at https://lccn.loc.gov/2019006310

Designer: Charmaine Whitman
Design Elements by Shutterstock

Printed and bound in the USA.
PA71

Table of Contents

Chapter 1
Winter Festival

Snow was falling—lots and lots of snow.

"Cool!" yelled Pedro. "Our winter festival will be a blast!"

Pedro met Katie at the park.

"Here comes Roddy with

a snowball," warned Katie.

"Duck!"

Pedro ducked, but he still

got hit.

"Come on!" said Katie.

"Let's enter the snowman

contest."

Katie made a snow whale.

Pedro made a snow horse.

It was a mess!

Roddy's snow dog was

the best.

Pedro said, "Let's sled

down the big hill. I'm a great

sledder!"

"Later," said Roddy. "First,

let's make snow angels."

Katie smiled. "Roddy and

angels do not go together!"

"For sure!" said Pedro.

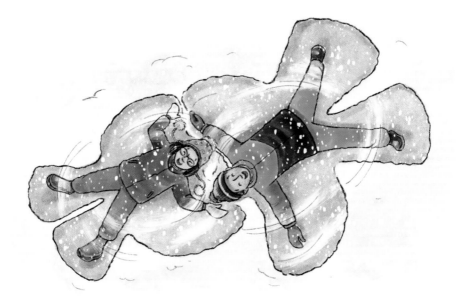

They plopped down in the
snow. Pedro said, "I know I can
make a perfect snow angel."

He didn't! But Pedro kept
his cool.

Chapter 2
Snowman and Skating

"Now let's sled down

the big hill," said Pedro.

"Later," said Roddy.

"I want to toss the hat

on the snowman."

Pedro tossed the hat.

He missed the snowman.

He missed over and over.

"No big deal," said Pedro.

Katie told Pedro, "Don't worry. Everyone is good at something. You are a great sledder."

"I am!" said Pedro.

"Let's go."

"See you later," said Roddy.

He began walking away.

"Wait!" said Pedro. "Why

don't you want to go sledding?"

Roddy looked at the hill.

Pedro looked at Roddy.

"That hill is high," said

Pedro. "Maybe it's a little

scary?"

"Maybe," said Roddy.

"Sledding can be scary at first," said Pedro. "But then it's cool."

He and Katie began walking up the hill. Roddy watched them.

Chapter 3
Blast Off!

"Wait!" Roddy began running after Pedro. "I want to try it. Can I ride with you?"

"Sure!" said Pedro. "Hop on and hold tight!"

Roddy held tight. He held

his breath too.

"Blast off!" yelled Pedro.

Whoosh!

They sped down the hill.

"Wow!" yelled Roddy.

"Wow, wow, WOW!"

"Awesome!" yelled Pedro.

"Let's do it again!" said

Roddy.

He told Pedro, "You are the best! That was so cool."

"Now let's hurry and have hot chocolate," said Pedro.

That was cool too!

About the Author

Fran Manushkin is the author of Katie Woo, the highly acclaimed fan-favorite early-reader series, as well as the popular Pedro series. Her other books include *Happy in Our Skin, Baby, Come Out!* and the best-selling board books *Big Girl Panties* and *Big Boy Underpants*. There is a real Katie Woo: Fran's great-niece, but she doesn't get into as much trouble as the Katie in the books. Fran lives in New York City, three blocks from Central Park, where she can often be found bird-watching and daydreaming. She writes at her dining room table, without the help of her naughty cats, Goldy and Chaim.

About the Illustrator

Tammie Lyon began her love for drawing at a young age while sitting at the kitchen table with her dad. She continued her love of art and eventually attended the Columbus College of Art and Design, where she earned a bachelor's degree in fine art. After a brief career as a professional ballet dancer, she decided to devote herself full time to illustration. Today she lives with her husband, Lee, in Cincinnati, Ohio. Her dogs, Gus and Dudley, keep her company as she works in her studio.

Glossary

awesome (AW-suhm)—extremely good

bragged (BRAGD)—talked in a boastful way about how good you are at something

breath (BRETH)—the air you take into your lungs and breathe out again

chocolate (CHOK-uh-lit)—a sweet food made from beans that grow on the tropical cacao tree

contest (KON-test)—an event where two or more people try to win something

festival (FESS-tuh-vuhl)—an organized set of events, often to celebrate and have fun

snow angel (SNOH AYN-gel)—a design made in fresh snow by lying on your back and moving your arms up and down and legs open and shut, to make the shape of a figure with wings

warned (WORND)—told someone about a danger or bad thing that may happen

Let's Talk

1. Talk about the ways the three friends help each other in this story.

2. What clues told Pedro that Roddy was nervous about sledding? Did you suspect there was a reason that Roddy kept suggesting other activities when sledding was suggested?

3. Pedro helps Roddy overcome his fear. Has a friend ever helped you overcome a fear? Talk about it.

Let's Write

1. Make a list of the activities at the winter festival. Circle your favorite one.

2. Pretend your school is hosting a winter festival, and you are in charge of the posters. Make a poster that tells everyone about the festival details.

3. Imagine you are sledding down a snowy hill. Write four sentences that explain what you see, feel, hear, and smell.

JOKE AROUND

❄ How does a snowman get to school?
by icicle

❄ What do snowmen say to greet each other?
"Ice to see you!"

❄ What did one snowman say to the other?
"Do you smell carrots?"

❄ What do you get when you cross a snowman with a vampire?
frostbite

WITH PEDRO!

❄ What do you call a snowman
temper tantrum?
a meltdown

❄ Where do snowmen go to dance?
the snowball

❄ What do snowmen have for
breakfast?
Frosted Snowflakes

❄ What often falls in the winter but
never gets hurt?
snow

HAVE MORE FUN WITH PEDRO!

PEDRO
THE BIG STINK
by FRAN MANUSHKIN

PEDRO
ON TOP OF THE WORLD
by FRAN MANUSHKIN

PEDRO
PEDRO'S BIG BREAK
by FRAN MANUSHKIN

PEDRO
PEDRO'S BIG GOAL
by FRAN MANUSHKIN

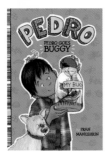
PEDRO
PEDRO GOES BUGGY
by FRAN MANUSHKIN

PEDRO
PEDRO GOES WILD!
by FRAN MANUSHKIN

PEDRO
PEDRO KEEPS HIS COOL
by FRAN MANUSHKIN

PEDRO
PEDRO'S MONSTER
by FRAN MANUSHKIN

PEDRO
PEDRO'S MYSTERY CLUB
by FRAN MANUSHKIN

PEDRO
PEDRO THE NINJA
by FRAN MANUSHKIN

PEDRO
PEDRO FOR PRESIDENT
by FRAN MANUSHKIN

PEDRO
PEDRO AND THE SHARK
by FRAN MANUSHKIN

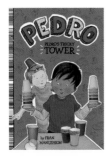
PEDRO
PEDRO'S TRICKY TOWER
by FRAN MANUSHKIN

PEDRO
PIRATE PEDRO
by FRAN MANUSHKIN